Busy Bees

by Margaretha Takmar

HOUGHTON MIFFLIN   BOSTON

Bee

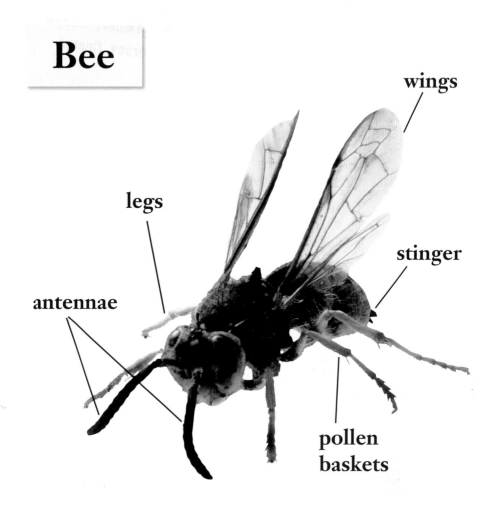

wings

legs

stinger

antennae

pollen
baskets

Bees are insects. They live almost everywhere in the world. Like other insects, bees have three pairs of legs. Unlike some bugs, bees have wings and antennae, or feelers.

Scientists think there are about 20,000 kinds of bees. Some bees live in groups called colonies. A colony may have between 20,000 and 80,000 bees!

A honeybee is one kind of bee.

Honeybees live in colonies. Each colony lives in a hive. Inside the hive, thousands of honeybees build a honeycomb.

The honeycomb has many holes called cells. Honeybees store food in some of the cells and raise babies in others.

How Bees Grow

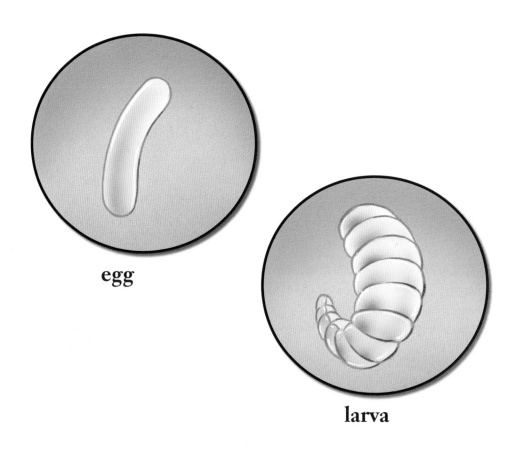

egg

larva

A queen bee lays an egg in some of the cells.
The eggs hatch into larvae. The larvae look like
worms. Worker bees care for and feed the larvae.

pupa

adult bee

Soon the larvae turn into pupae. Slowly, the pupae turn into honeybees. Then they climb out of their cells.

Bees eat nectar and pollen. Both these things come from flowering plants.

Bees sip sweet nectar with their long tongues. When the bees get back to their hive, they spit up the nectar. They give it to other bees or store it in cells. Later, the nectar turns to honey. Bees also mix nectar with pollen to make bee bread. They feed the bee bread to growing bees.

Bees spread pollen from one flower to another. They help plants make seeds.

Some bees collect pollen in pollen baskets. Pollen baskets are not real baskets. They are smooth patches on a bee's back legs. Long, curved hairs surround the patches. Bees stuff grains of pollen into their pollen baskets. When the pollen baskets are full, they look like yellow bumps.

Bumblebees have bands of yellow and black.

Bumblebees live in colonies too. Unlike honeybees, bumblebees do not live in hives. Instead, they build nests in clumps of grass or in holes in the ground.

carpenter bee

Other kinds of bees live alone. They do not live in colonies. Carpenter bees and leaf-cutting bees are two kinds of bees that live alone.

Carpenter bees make their nests in wood or in plant stems. They can chew round tunnels in branches, telephone poles, and even houses.

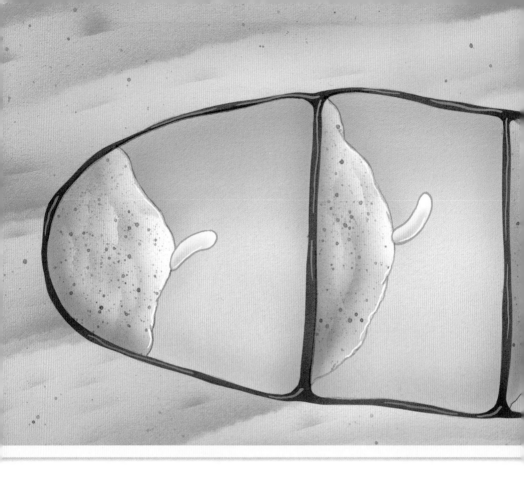

The carpenter bee puts some bee bread at the end of its tunnel. Next, the carpenter bee lays an egg on top of the bee bread. Then she seals the egg into the tunnel. The carpenter bee keeps working until the tunnel is filled with cells.

The eggs soon turn into larvae. The larvae eat the bee bread and become pupae.

The cells are like cocoons. Inside the cells, the pupae change to adult bees. Then they chew their way out of their cells and fly away.

Leaf-cutting bees also make their nests in tunnels. Sometimes they dig round holes in branches or underground. Then they line their tunnels with pieces of leaves from bushes or other plants.

Leaf-cutting bees cut holes in these leaves.

Bees have many enemies. Skunks, birds, dragonflies, wasps, flies, and other bugs like to eat bees. People also kill bees.

Bears and some ants wreck beehives to eat the honey that they find inside. Some bees sting their enemies to defend their nests and themselves.

All the different kinds of bees are important to our natural world. Three cheers for busy bees!